Auntie

by Elise

Claus

Primavera

SCHOLASTIC INC.

New York Toronto London Auckland Sydney Mexico City New Delhi Hong Kong

THE KRINGLE FAMILY lived high
atop the luxurious Bing Cherry Hotel in
New York City, and they loved Christmas.
They kept a Christmas tree up all year round.
Mr. Kringle was president of the renowned
Jingle Bell Bell Company. Mrs. Kringle owned
the fabulous Mistle-Toe-to-Nail Salon over on
56th and Fifth. They had even named their
young son after you-know-who.

Sophie and her little brother had everything. But if you asked
was it enough, "No!" they would say. Was it enough to have their
own private soda fountain? "No!" They would shake their heads back and
forth. Or clothes and books galore? "No! No! No!" they would scream.

It had been suggested by their great-aunt, Auntie Claus, that maybe Sophie and her little brother were given *too* many presents.

"You can never have *too* many presents," sniffed Sophie. "That's my motto!"

Yes, everyone in the Kringle family loved Christmas, but no one loved it more than Auntie Claus. Auntie Claus lived at the Bing as well—penthouse 25C. Every afternoon Sophie was summoned there for tea.

Each day Auntie Claus would instruct Sophie on a different topic. One day it might be Christmas trees—"Always pick a nice full one, darling, with springy needles."

Another day, decorating—"You must dr-a-a-ape the garland, darling, one strand at a time; you must never t-h-r-o-o-o-w it on!"

After they finished tea, Auntie Claus would close with these words of wisdom, "And darling, always remember my first and final rule—whether it's birthdays, Christmas, or Halloween, it is far better to give than it is to receive!"

Sophie wondered about her great-aunt a lot.

She's so *mysterioso*! Sophie thought. And this was true.

There were many strange goings-on up in penthouse 25C. Most people considered Auntie Claus just another eccentric New Yorker. But Sophie knew that there was more to her than met the eye. For instance, what was the diamond key that always hung from a silver ribbon around her neck?

"Just a bit of costume jewelry, darling," her great-aunt would say, then quickly change the subject.

Why did Auntie Claus leave every year right after Halloween and not return until Valentine's Day?

"Just a business trip, darling," and she'd change the subject again.

Where does she go? Sophie wanted to know.

Once again it was Halloween, and Auntie Claus announced: "In one week, I'm off on my annual business trip!"

"What kind of business are you in, anyway?" Sophie had asked.

"That, darling, is something for me to know and you to find out," Auntie Claus had said with a twinkle in her eye.

And that was exactly what Sophie intended to do. "This year I have a plan—I'll stow away!" Sophie had made up her mind.

As she was leaving, Sophie said, "I'm going on a business trip with Auntie Claus."

"Marvelous, darling. Be home in time for Christmas—there's a good girl," said her mother.

"Do take your mittens!" said her father.

"I'm going, too!" said her little brother.

"Oh no you're not!" said Sophie.

"Can if I want to!" he said.

"Can NOT!" she said.

"Can TOO!" he cried.

"CANNOT!" she yelled.

"W-A-A-A-A-A-H-H-H!!!"

Sophie could hear his earsplitting scream start to fade as she ran out the door.

Sophie tiptoed into Auntie Claus's apartment. There were many boxes and trunks waiting to go. Choosing the largest, Sophie pushed aside the capes and furs, and wriggled inside. Quietly she made a little peephole in the cardboard, so she could see everything that was going on.

Auntie Claus entered the room. She removed the diamond key that hung from the ribbon around her neck. Next she placed the key into the lock of her old elevator. The door slid open. The boxes and trunks were loaded. The door slid shut.

VROOM! The elevator shot up in the air and out into space. They were going up-Up-UP! Minutes . . . an hour passed, and still they were going up.

Sophie could feel it getting colder and colder. From her peephole she could see stars zipping by, or was that snow? We can't possibly be in New York any longer, she thought.

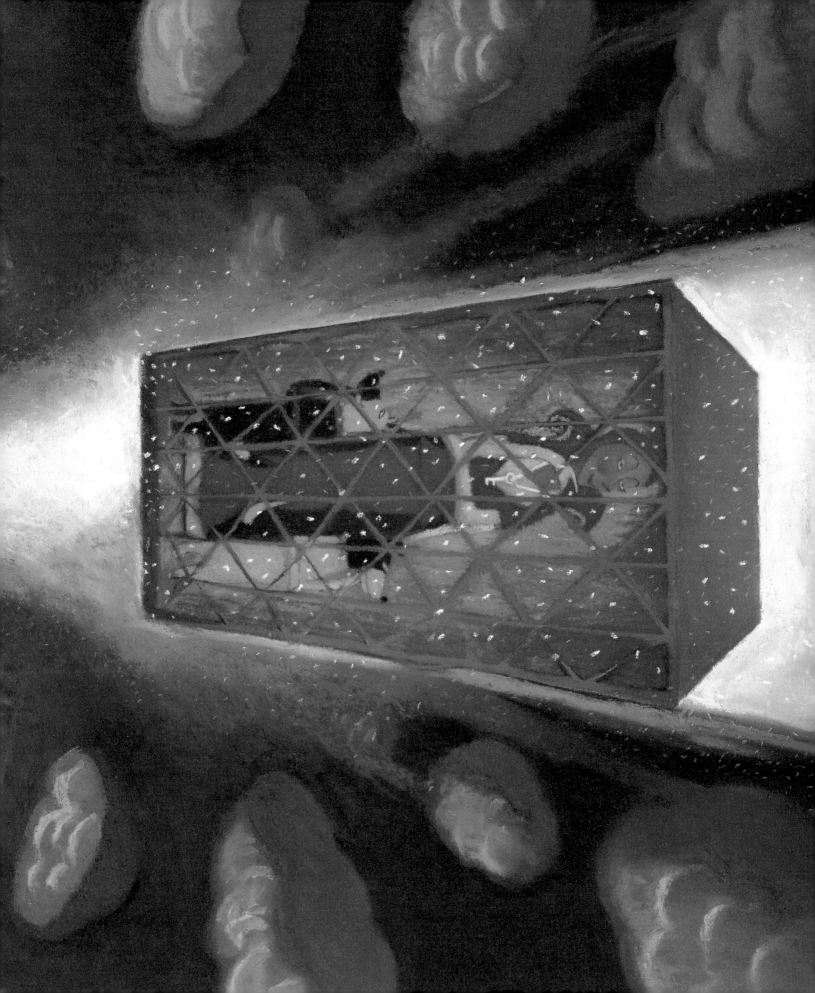

The elevator landed with a *thunk*, tipping over Sophie's box. She could no longer see, but she thought she heard cheers.

The sound soon faded until all became completely
silent. Thinking it safe, she climbed out of the box.
"Where am I?" Sophie whispered.

"You must be the new elf," a little man said.

"That's it," said Sophie. "I'm the new elf. Who are you?"

"I'm Mr. Pudding," he said. "Oh dear, oh dear, you're in violation of Elf Rule Number Three."

"What do you mean?" asked Sophie indignantly.

He pulled a worn green-and-red book from his pocket. On the cover it read: ELF RULES AND VITAL INFORMATION. He pointed to the section marked Dress Code.

Sophie read out loud: "'Always look neat, always look snappy; a well-dressed elf always feels happy.'"

"Follow me!" he said, and trotted off into the darkness.

"Where are we going?" shouted Sophie.

"Hurry! Hurry!" Mr. Pudding called over his shoulder. "Only forty-eight days left!"

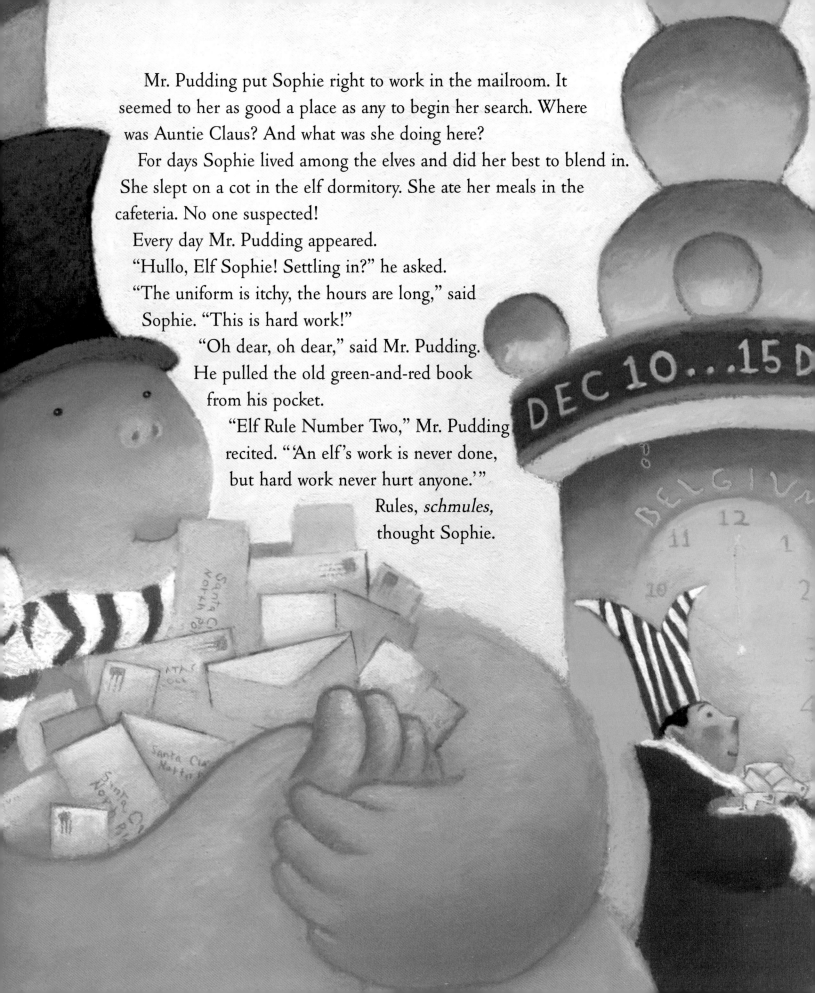

Mr. Pudding put Sophie right to work in the mailroom. It seemed to her as good a place as any to begin her search. Where was Auntie Claus? And what was she doing here?

For days Sophie lived among the elves and did her best to blend in. She slept on a cot in the elf dormitory. She ate her meals in the cafeteria. No one suspected!

Every day Mr. Pudding appeared.

"Hullo, Elf Sophie! Settling in?" he asked.

"The uniform is itchy, the hours are long," said Sophie. "This is hard work!"

"Oh dear, oh dear," said Mr. Pudding. He pulled the old green-and-red book from his pocket.

"Elf Rule Number Two," Mr. Pudding recited. "'An elf's work is never done, but hard work never hurt anyone.'"

Rules, *schmules*, thought Sophie.

For weeks Sophie looked high and low for Auntie Claus, but now it was almost Christmas Eve and she had turned up nothing. Sophie was worried. If she didn't find Auntie Claus, how would she get home?... If she didn't get home... How will I get all my Christmas presents? she thought.

Just then Mr. Pudding appeared.

"Hullo, Elf Sophie," he said. "Good news! You have excelled in the mailroom and may proceed to package wrapping. After that we'll all pitch in on sleigh packing."

"I'm not going to package wrapping and I'm not going to sleigh packing. I want to go home!" Sophie yelled. "I have to get all my —"

But before she could finish, Santa's voice interrupted over the P.A. system.

Yes, a brave elf, thought Sophie, or else a girl who thinks she might be on that list. She raised her hand high. "I'll go!" she said.

"Oh dear, oh dear," Mr. Pudding said.

As Sophie made her way toward the coal mines, she could hear the chanting of the B-B-and-G elves:

"Spoiled brats and crybabies, whine babies, and all the ones who don't believe: Here's some coal and here's some gunk— fill a stocking that smells like skunk!"

Sophie went down, down, down where it became darker and darker.

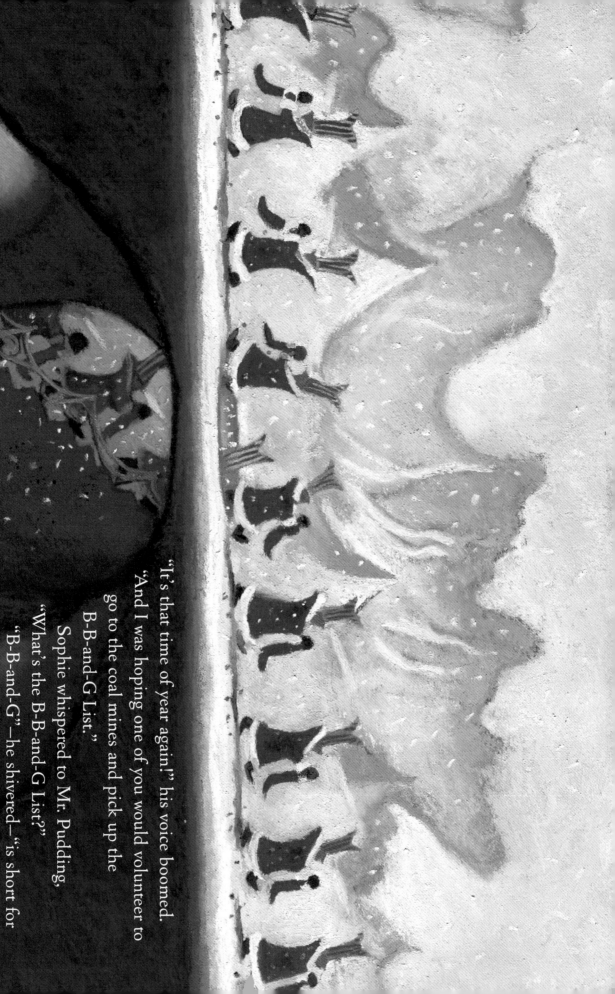

"It's that time of year again!" his voice boomed.

"And I was hoping one of you would volunteer to go to the coal mines and pick up the B-B-and-G List."

Sophie whispered to Mr. Pudding, "What's the B-B-and-G List?"

"B-B-and-G"—he shivered—"is short for Bad-Boys-and-Girls. Any boy or girl on that list goes without presents—or worse—for Christmas!"

Sophie swallowed hard. Uh-oh, she thought. Mr. Pudding continued, "Only the bravest elf would volunteer for such an awful job."

Finally she reached the very bottom. There was the list! Sophie looked for her name. But it wasn't her name she saw on the list. It was…

"My own little brat of a brother!" she cried. "Chris is on the Bad-Boys-and-Girls List!"

Well, she thought, once she'd gotten past the shock of it, they do kind of have a point. But then she pictured the two of them on Christmas morning. There would be lots of presents for her and nothing for her little brother. On his favorite day of the year, Chris would find only a stinky stocking filled with coal and gunk. "He will be so disappointed…. He will be so sad," Sophie said. She quickly erased his name, but now there was a large telltale gap.

There was only one thing to do.

Sophie took a deep breath and wrote down her *own* name instead.

The ink wasn't even dry on the page when some kind of really strong magic happened.

Right before her eyes, the list, the B-B-and-G elves, and the coal mines vanished, and Sophie was whirling around and around, hurling through the air in a blur of Christmas red and green. Was she up? Was she down?

Sophie was standing on the stage in the Grand Ballroom. A clock struck midnight.

Santa began to speak. "She's always on time, she works harder than anyone I know—including me. Ho, ho, ho! In short, she does things right and I would be lost without her. Let's have a big round of applause for my sister...."

The curtain opened.

"Auntie Claus!" Sophie shouted.

"Auntie Claus!" everybody cheered. "Hooray for Auntie Claus!!"

Turning to Sophie, Auntie Claus winked and said, "Come along, darling, you must be home in time for Christmas!"

Sophie was about to climb onto the sleigh when Mr. Pudding appeared. He was waving the green-and-red book in the air. "Oh dear, oh dear!" he cried. "Auntie Claus, Sophie can't leave until she knows the first and final rule—see, it says so right here under Departing Procedures!"

The reindeer stomped restlessly and shook their heads as if to say, Let's go, let's go!

"Sophie knows the first and final rule, Mr. Pudding," Auntie Claus said.

"I do?" said Sophie.

"Yes, you do. Now hop onto the sleigh—there's a good girl."

Sophie jumped onto the sleigh, and it rose up into the sky.
"Good-bye! Good-bye!" she called. She could barely hear her aunt's
voice over the wind and the snow.
"I knew you had it in you. Merry Christmas, darling!"

The sleigh picked up speed.
"Ho! Ho! Ho!" Santa laughed as the stars whizzed by.
Sophie closed her eyes. Her face stung with
the cold.

When Sophie opened her eyes, she could hardly believe
she was in her own bed again. She ran down the stairs,
toward the living room. "Please, let him get his
presents," she whispered to herself.

Under the tree was her little brother. His cheeks were red, his eyes
sparkled, his belly shook with laughter.

"Merry Christmas, Sophie!" he bellowed.

"Merry Christmas, Chris," Sophie said with great relief. It was then
that she realized: Auntie Claus is right. I *do* know the first and final rule.
She said to herself, "It is far better
to give than it is to receive!"

"There is something here for you," her mother and
father said proudly. They handed Sophie a tiny
box with a card. Inside was a diamond key hanging
from a red ribbon.
"It's from Auntie Claus," Sophie said.
"Where is Auntie Claus, anyway?" Chris piped up.

"On a business trip, darling!". Sophie said, and smiled mysteriously.
Suddenly a thought occurred to Chris. "She's never here on
Christmas," he said. "What kind of business is she in, anyway?"

"That is something for me to know and you to find out," Sophie said
to her little butterball of a brother.

And someday he would...but that's another story.

For my mother and father,
the original Kringles!
—E. P.

ISBN 0-439-21886-1

Copyright © 1999 Elsie Primavera.
All rights reserved.
Published by Scholastic Inc., 555 Broadway, New York, NY 10012,
by arrangementwith Harcourt, Brace & Company.
SCHOLASTIC and associated logos are trademarks and/or registered
trademarks of Scholastic Inc.

12 11 10 9 8 7 6 5 4 3 2   0 1 2 3 4 5/0

Printed in the U.S.A.   14

First Scholastic printing, September 2000

The illustrations were done in gouache and pastel
on illustration board treated with gesso.
The display type was hand lettered by Geoegia Deaver.
The text type was set in Cloister.
Designed by Camilla Filancia and Ivan Holmes.

Auntie Claus
NEW YORK   NORTH POLE

For my dear niece Sophie,
    You really are a chip off
the old block!
                    Love,
P.S.   Auntie Claus
I'll be expecting you for tea on Valentine's Day darling...